To:

TO GET RID OF A ZOMBIE!

Love your Zombie!

WRITTEN BY LYLE PEREZ-TINICS
ILLUSTRATED BY APRIL GUADIANA

Rainstorm Press
PO BOX 391038
Anza, Ca 92539
www.RainstormPress.com

ISBN 10 - 1-937758-21-4
ISBN 13 - 978-1-937758-21-9

Library of Congress: 2012907827

25 WAYS TO GET RID OF A ZOMBIE
Rainstorm Press

Interior design by -
The Mad Formatter
www.TheMadFormatter.com

Cover illustration by April Guadiana

Praise for
25 WAYS TO GET RID OF A ZOMBIE

"Just when you thought it was safe to sleep, having learned all the ways to get rid of a zombie, Lyle Perez-Tinics messes it all up by giving you another 25 ways to get rid of a zombie."

- Tony Faville, author of ***Kings of the Dead***

"Grab a friend, family member or your pet zombie. Curl up next to a warm fire and get ready for some gut bursting, head exploding, zombieriffic laughter. With ***25 Ways to get rid of a Zombie***, Lyle Perez-Tinics has created the ultimate zombie execution manual. You have to read this. It may save your life."

- Nate D. Burleigh, author of ***Sustenance***

"LMFAO!!!! Within 2 seconds of getting this book I was already rolling when I looked through the Table of Contents."

- Etienne DeForest, author of ***The Zombie Survival Guide: How to Live Like a King After the Outbreak***

"The only problem I see with this book is that it doesn't come with diapers, because I just shit my pants! Very Funny."

- Alan Gandy, author of ***Voyeur Dead***

OTHER WORKS BY
LYLE PEREZ-TINICS

Existing Dead

Dement

Death's Too Short

The Undead That Saved Christmas:
Vol. 1 & 2 and Vampire Edition

Disclaimer:

This book is only to be taken lightly and something you can laugh at. Zombies, have not, are not, will not be real in any way, shape, or form. Within these pages you will see foul and absurd language that should not be taken offensively. Words are just that, words. They were not included in this text to hurt or upset anyone, but to be laughed at. If you are easily offended by the use of the words, fuck, bitch, whore, asshole, cunt, douche, ect ... please do not read this book. But if you are the type of person that can laugh at bad language and obscure images, continue reading. I wrote this book for you.

Dedication:

To those of us who can take a joke.

To Bill Hinzman, who was the model for our zombie friend. Rest in piece.

25 WAYS TO GET RID OF A ZOMBIE

*Introduction

I'M WITH ZOMBIE

INTRODUCTION

So, you have a zombie you need to get rid of. What are you gonna do? Where are you gonna take it? Your wife has had enough living with the creature. The smell is awful, the dogs are always pissing on the carpet because their scared of it, the kids are learning bad zombie habits, and who knows what the hell happened to the mail man. Your wife is fed up and she says that it's time for that "thing" to go. You can't exactly take your zombie companion to the nearest homeless shelter ... Or can you?

Within this guide you will learn 25 creative ways to getting rid of your pesky (but loveable) zombie. But be warned, there is no clear cut way to get rid of one of the undead. As you will see there are consequences for most situations. Whichever way you decide to rid yourself from your zombie is entirely up to you, just be ready to suffer the consequences.

#1
EAT THEIR BRAIN

Since the 1980's zombies have been eating brains 'til they're faces turned gray. That's all you see now-a-days, zombies eating brains at the market, zombies eating brains in a payphone, zombies eating brains while getting a lap dance and so on. I think it's about time someone gave zombies a taste of their own medicine. The Chinese have been steaming monkey heads and eating their brains for years. Do the same with your zombie. Tell it that *you're* going to cook a little znack and while it's waiting at the breakfast nook, grab a saw or axe, whatever you prefer, and hack off the cunt's head. Make sure you have a steam pot going. Don't freak out when the severed head's eyes move about. It's perfectly normal. You haven't destroyed the brain, so technically they're still alive err ... umm ... undead. Place the head into the pot and cook it for about two hours or until tender. Don't forget to dispose of the other body parts by mixing them in with your regular trash. Make sure you hide them well or else you'll scare the shit out of the garbage man and have the cops knocking at your door. When the head is ready, take it out of the pot (caution HOT!) remove the scalp and grab a fork!

Not all zombies eat with a fork and knife.

The eyeball is the juiciest.

As appealing as this method might seem, not just to me but to everyone, it's not recommended. Not only will it leave a huge mess, but it will more than likely infect you with the zombie virus, and believe me, that's worse then an STD. Not to mention, if your wife found out you ate zombie brains , she'll never kiss you again or worse, never let you lick her dark tunnel if you know what I mean. Eating a zombie's brain will be the ultimate revenge (if one ate the brains of a loved one) but in the end, you'll be screwed and just another undead cunt.

#2
THROW IT INTO A VOLCANO

You have to destroy the brain in order to kill a zombie, right? Well, why stop there? Why not just destroy the whole fucking thing? Throwing the zombie into a volcano is hard work, but it is also a great way to insure the zombie is destroyed. First you have to locate an active volcano, trust me there are a lot of them. Second, you have to get the zombie there without it catching wind. While you're driving make sure to buckle up (safety first) and roll down the windows. Being in an enclosed area with a zombie could make you pass out. When you arrive at the volcano, you'll have to fling the zombie over your shoulders in a fireman's carry. Take your time and slowly walk to the top. Make sure the zombie is blindfolded, it might freak out if it knew it was about to die ... again. It might have flashbacks. When you reach the top, say your goodbyes, and toss it over. You might not be able to see much depending on the ash and smoke. But rest assured that your zombie is no more.

Fireman's carry.
Dramatization, I'm too lazy to actually do it.

"I didn't do it."

The only thing you'll need to be worried about is if throwing the zombie into the volcano somehow triggers an eruption. The chances of this happening are minimal but still, if zombies can exists then why can't a volcano erupt while you're near it? When the deed is done and you're walking back to your car make sure to stop and feel for vibrations. If there's a rumbling at your feet, run like hell! But if you're already far away, act like you had nothing to do with it.

#3
TAKE IT TO AN OPERA

A night at the opera can be a wonderful experience. It's one of the only events where you can dress up and listen to people sing notes you didn't know were possible. I've heard that some singers can hit a pitch that will shatter glass. Getting ideas? I am. Dress your zombie in its best Monkey Suit and take the entire family out to the opera. Bring plastic bags because when the zombie's head explodes, it'll make a mess.

Zombies enjoy operas almost as much as humans. See?

Triple whammy, the glass shattered as well.

Unless you're into opera music, I don't suggest you attempt this one. The chances of a high pitched scream causing the zombies head to explode is again, at a minimal. The chances of you dying of boredom are very high. This plan might backfire and you'll end up dead. Or who knows, you might get a double whammy, you'll die of boredom and the zombie's head will explode.

#4 ABANDONMENT

We've all thought about doing this with unwanted house pets that shit on our beds or piss in our shoes. Most of us will do it the humane way and take these pests to our local pet shelter. Of course, we all claim that we 'found' the critter so we don't have to pay the fee. Others wouldn't want to go through that hassle and would rather take the dog, the cat, the gorilla, whatever, to the backyard and blow its brains out, (we'll get to that later.) For zombies, there are no shelters to take them to. When you need to get rid of the beast, you gotta do it the old fashion way. Grab your blind fold and the zombie 'cause it's time to go for a ride. If you can spare the gas, I suggest you take the zombie as far out as you can. Find a dumpster in an alley or just head for the desert. You don't even have to stop the car, just open the passenger side door and kick that nuisance out.

Watch it fly!

For zombies, too much sun is a bad thing.

Zombies have been known to track humans by scent. In time, if a zombie gets accustom to a certain human's smell, that zombie can track the individual for hundreds of miles. If you're planning on abandoning your zombie, expect a knock on the door five, ten, maybe fifteen years later by a tired, pissed off zombie. Duck when it swings at you.

#5
HOMELESS SHELTER

These places seem to be everywhere. It's the perfect environment for a zombie. Most of the people there already smell, and even look like the living dead. One more body into the mix won't bother anyone. First thing you do is look in the phone book and find a homeless shelter. Call them to find out when they serve dinner. When you get all the information, you move on to the next step. You gotta get the zombie down there. Make sure you show up when there are a lot of homeless people around, that way you can just shove the zombie into the room and walk away slowly. He'll blend right in.

Blends right in.

Bum Fights II

One of the many dangers you'll come across with homeless people is that they are crazy. Look at them the wrong way and they might kick your ass. Thanks to Bum Fights, these real bums think they can go around kicking ass for some booze. With that in mind, once you drop off the zombie don't look back. If you find yourself getting mugged by a bum, run to your zombie and turn him loose. Of course, if it hasn't caught on to what you were doing, it'll come to your defense. But if your zombie is smart, it'll look the other way, leaving you to have to fight off a horde of bums.

#6
FIRE

This would be a great idea if you lived in the desert. Just drench the poor cunt in gas and set him ablaze. Of course, if you have to be discrete about it, I recommend going to the desert with a handful of people. Everyone loves burning wood pallets in one huge fire, and people enjoy drinking a lot. When everyone is wasted, you carefully take the zombie out of your vehicle and push him in the fire. Zombie's hate fire, so remember the blindfold! When the beast is in the fire, grab a bat and smash him with it 42 times exactly. (Close your eyes cause the smoke hurts!) You'll be tired yes, but it has to be done. It's been tested and 42 blows by a bat will stop a zombie. Now make sure it turns to ashes and you're free from the zombie.

42 Times!

I hate my life.

I recommend going with a group of people because after the deed is done, you'll wanna relax and have a good time. Maybe drink a couple dozen beers 'til you can't shut up about how much you miss your zombie friend. You might even think about how much your life sucks, how your wife controls EVERYTHING you do and then jump into the fire yourself. You'll need the other people around to stop you from jumping in. So yeah, burning a zombie = to much drama = bad idea. And besides have you ever smelled a burning body? It's not pleasant.

#7
THE HEADSHOT

This is one of the most common ways to kill a zombie. In every zombie movie you watch, the zombies are being shot left and right. Don't be a copy cat, think of another way to get rid of your zombie. Fine! If you're so hung on shooting the zombie in the head here's how you do it. Purchase a rifle, or handgun, whatever you can get from your local pawnshop. Grab your zombie and take it to the back yard. Tie its hands behind its back and drop it to its knees. Take a few steps back, aim your firearm at the side of its head and squeeze, not pull, the trigger. If blood and brain matter fly everywhere you did a good job.

Got to remember the BLINDFOLD!

Pow, right in the kisser!

You may be thinking, what can go wrong with a good clean shot to the head? Well, you may have gotten the zombie, but you're too stupid to notice the metal trashcans behind it. The bullet will ricochet off of them and get you right in the head. That's what you get for being so unoriginal.

#8
BURY IT UNDEAD

It just seems so easy doesn't it? Digging a large hole and tossing the zombie in it. That's basically all you have to do to bury a zombie. Well, besides looking for a place to do it. Just keep it simple and use your backyard. Use it as an excuse to get rid of that fucking stupid garden your wife says she's going to continue but never does. If only it were that easy ...

In my dreams would I ever dig a hole this size.

Fucking garden.

Have you ever dug a large hole? It's fucking tiring. All you have is a shovel, you're credit is so fucked up you can't go rent a bobcat. As easy as this one may seem, I'm too lazy to dig a hole and I'm sure you are too. Of course, you can always pay a day laborer to do it. But then you'll have to explain to your wife why twenty bucks is missing from her purse and who this guy next to you is. It's like you're a fucking child. On the plus side, if a zombie is buried in the backyard it'll taint the soil so nothing will grow. Bye bye fucking garden.

#9
GIVE IT AWAY TO SCIENCE

Scientists are always looking for fresh zombie's to experiment on. Did I say scientists? Yeah, I mean mad, fucking Frankenstein scientists. It's just so easy to drive up to the laboratory, knock on the door and take off running. If you wanna be funny, dress the zombie up in baby clothes and hand it a bottle. When the mad scientist takes the zombie into his lab your hands are free. Just don't feel bad when you start thinking about your zombie in bondage, tied up to a bed with its ass sticking in the air.

I love this joke.

***Scene from** The Back Rotting Door V.*

Don't be stupid. Don't give up your zombie to these assholes. You know the only thing they want them for is sex slaves. Avoid these "scientists" at all cost. Unless you're as sick as these cutns, then you might see this as an opportunity for zombie porn. Grab your camera and start filming away you sicko.

#10
BLAST IT INTO SPACE

This idea will take some work. First you gotta learn rocket science. You know how that idiom goes, "It's not rocket science," when something is not so hard? People say that because rocket science IS hard. Unless you know how to build a rocket or know someone who does, this method will be a massive failure. You can always buy one of those kid rockets, but I don't think that'll work. Your best bet is to head down to Florida and duct tape the bastard to the side of the space shuttle. Yeah, good luck with that one; however, if you're dedicated, and have connections, I can see the zombie getting taped to the side of the space shuttle. Wave as the rocket, and your zombie, blasts into orbit.

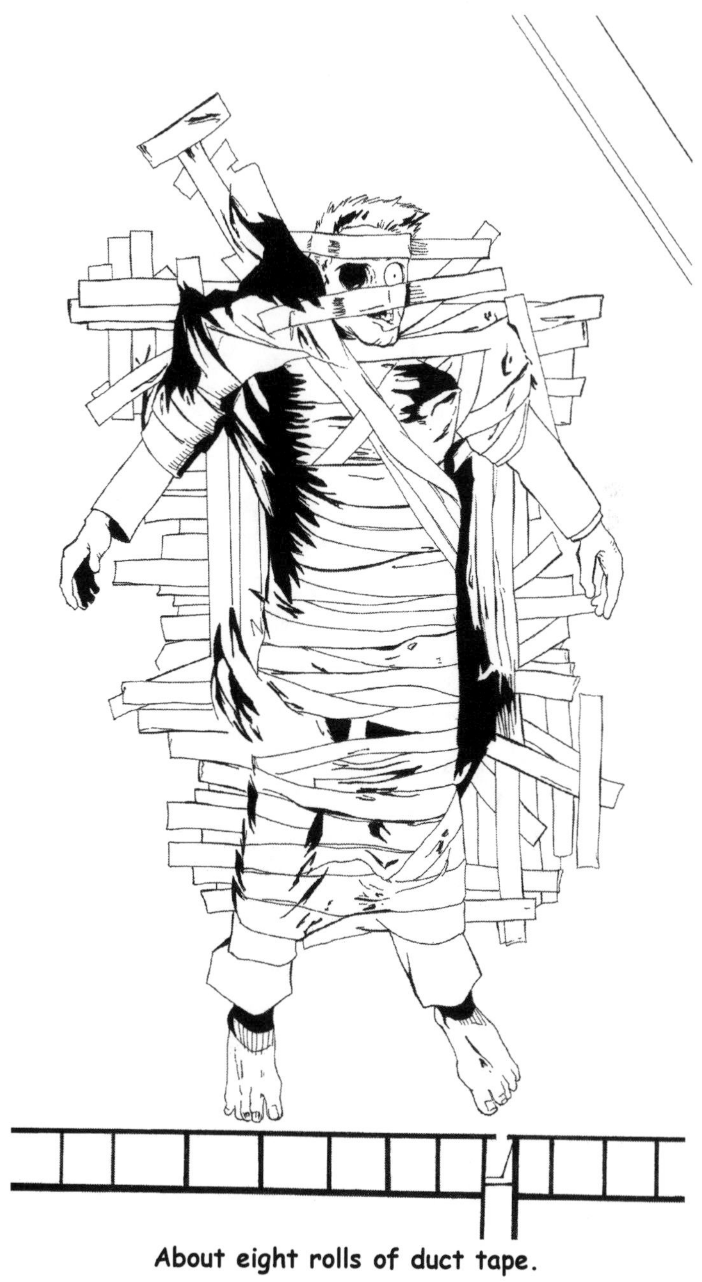

About eight rolls of duct tape.

Brrraaaiiiinnnnssss ...

Make sure you run because when that rocket fails and explodes in the sky, there's going to be infected zombie juice everywhere. I recommend you run and hide in a large building. When the zombie's liquefied body sprays everywhere and infects anyone that comes into contact with it, you can remain unscathed. If you can live with thousands of human reanimations on your conches, then be my guest and try to blast your zombie into space.

#11
TAXIDERMY

For some reason, people frown on the art of taxidermy. I don't know why, it looks like a nifty idea. Let's say you've had a dog since it was a puppy. The dog is now 15 and as senile as your 100-year-old grandmother. Stupid (the dog) craps everywhere, he can hardly move let alone fuck anymore. It jumps in front of your car in hopes you'd end its miserable life. You wanna keep Stupid with you forever, well taxidermy has made this possible. What better way to get rid of your zombie then by stuffing it with ... whatever the fuck these people use and keeping it in your game room.

Mans best friends.

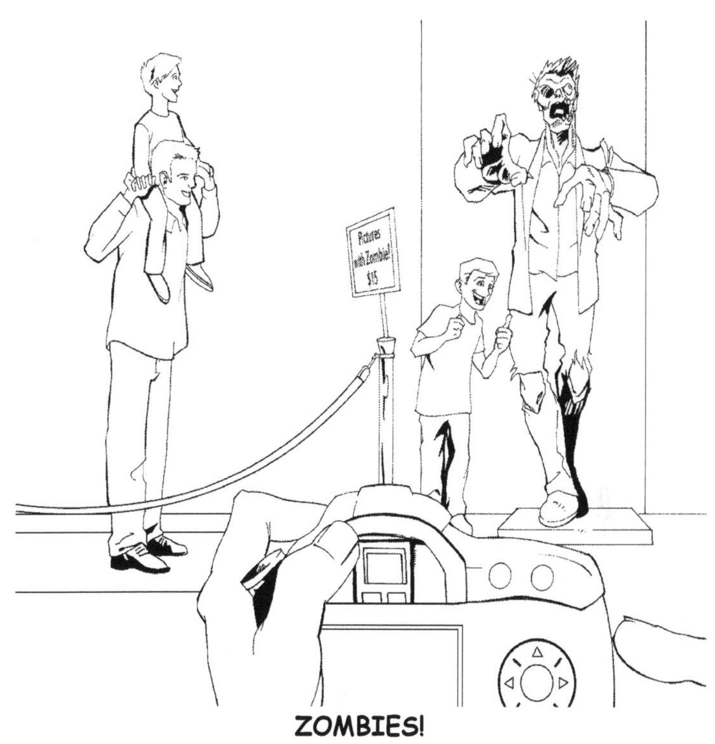

ZOMBIES!
Bringing families together since 2012.

I really don't see anything bad with this one. Make sure you have the taxidermist leave the zombie in a horrifying pose. Who knows, you might even be able to charge people five bucks to take pictures next to it. Oh wait, what if your wife tells you she wants that gone too? I'll tell you one thing, if you start thinking that there's room for a taxidermy version of her next to the zombie, you better go for a drive. One more thing, good luck finding a taxidermist that would do a fucking zombie, trust me I looked.

#12
STONING

It worked in the bible. Just get a lynch mob all fired up and accuse the zombie of being a witch. After the trial, make sure you yell out stoning as a way of execution. When the execution is taken outside grab some rocks and get the party started. No one will suspect that the zombie is yours and if anyone does just deny.

"Get that witch cunt!"

Matching t-shirts for sale, only $19.99!

If by any chance denying doesn't work, just run away. You'll get a good jog while you regret ever buying those matching human / zombie t-shirts. If by any chance your zombie outruns you, you might want to consider going to the gym from time to time.

#13
ELECTRIC SHOCK

Have you ever stuck a fork into an electrical socket? I haven't because I was never the 'stupid' one in my circle of friends. I have seen a lot of people do it, though. There's a big shock and a little puff of smoke then the person usually drops the folk before any real damage happens. I've heard stories that electric shock could cause someone's head to explode. I've never witnessed that, but I sure would like to see someone try it with their zombie. Use the best invention ever created, duct tape, and tape the fork around the zombie's hand. Be sure to use a wooden stick to help guide the zombies hand to the socket. When it's in, just watch and see what happens.

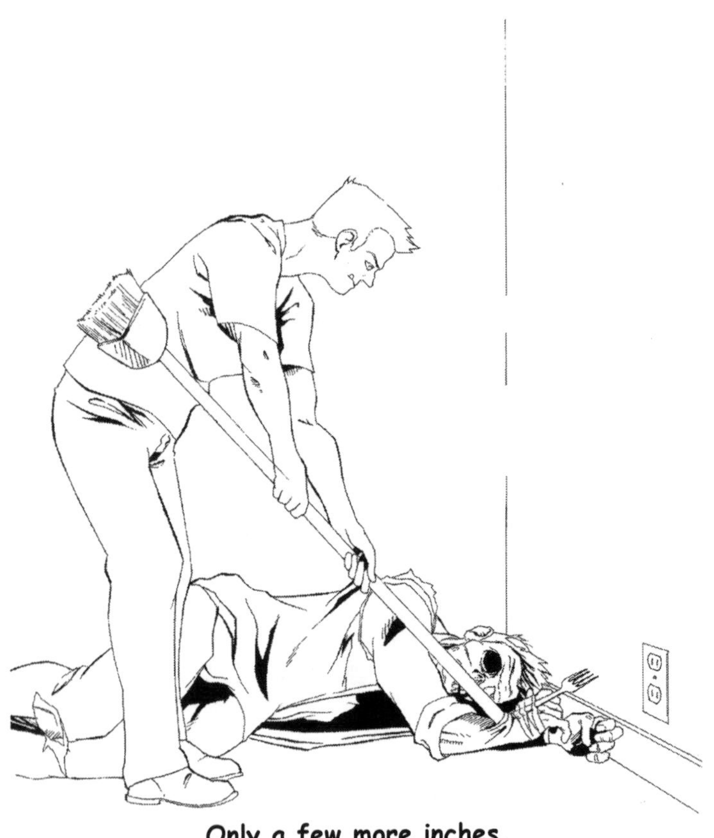

Only a few more inches.

It's just like Christmas.

Best case scenario is that it works and the zombies head explodes. Worst case, you blow a breaker and the entire town goes into a blackout. What am I saying? If the power goes out in the whole town it's a good thing. If you're zombie friend is still undead, grab 'em because it's time to start looting.

#14
FRAME IT FOR A CRIME

Believe it or not, framing a zombie for a crime is very simple. Most people in the world would love to just lock up these cunts and throw away the key. I myself love zombies, I have no problems with them. I'm just trying to teach the reader how to get rid of it before the Mrs. says, "no sex until that thing is gone." Sorry zombie dudes, but if it's zombies or having sex, sex will win all the time. Unless you're a sicko that has intercourse with zombies, if that's the case close this book and try to get your money back. Good luck with that. Okay, framing the zombie. You can do this multiple ways, but for example, we'll use something simple like stealing. All you need to do is walk into a store with your zombie. Make sure it has a back pack on. Once you're in the store, find a corner and just start filling the bag with random stuff. When the backpack is full, zip it up and continue walking. Tell your zombie friend to go to the car to get your wallet. When it walks through the door and the alarms go off, hide in the bathroom.

Freeze one eyed motherfucker!

Take her. She smells worst than you down there.

There are a few possible outcomes to this, you come out of the restroom and learn from an employee that a zombie was shoplifting and the cops took it away. You come out of the restroom and there's a bloody mess everywhere, limbs and other body part will littler the ground. And in the middle of the carnage there will be one very pissed off zombie. Another outcome is that the cops will find out the zombie is your responsibility and end up taking your ass to jail. If that last one happens, be prepared to get a visit from your wife and the zombie. When she tells you that she's leaving you for the zombie, just accept it. Call her a fucking rot lover and be done with it.

#15
PLAY FRISBEE WITH CIRCULAR SAW BLADES

The zombie will never know what hit it. Tell your zombie friend you wanna go to the park to play Frisbee. Who doesn't like Frisbee? Before you go to the park make sure you stop by your local hardware store to pick up some circular saw blades. When you're at the park make sure you stand a good twenty feet away from the zombie. When the blades start flying, you don't want to be anywhere near the splatter zone.

"Just a little more to the right."

Perfect time for a *Home Alone* reenactment.

One thing you have to worry about with this method is how terrible your aim is. You're trying to get the zombies head, not its arms or its legs and especially not an innocent bystander. If you end up hitting someone that was just walking by, go back to the previous way to get rid of your zombie and blame the incident on it. When the cops show up, I suggest you hand all of the blades to the zombie and take off running.

#16
PUSH IT OFF A TALL BUILDING

This one sounds easy, right? All you need to do is find access to the roof of a tall building and push the zombie off the edge. Most zombies won't know what's going on but if you got one of those smart ones, it's going to catch on. It might even try to grab a hold of you. If you need assistance I advise using a long pole. If you decide on the pole make sure you find one before you go on the roof. You won't find much of anything up there. Also, prepare to look a fucking fool walking up to the roof with a zombie and a large pole.

Go over godammit!

Shit. Not again.

If you don't feel like using a pole or you can't find one, pushing them off the ledge bare handed is the only way to go. Just don't push so hard or else you'll lose your balance and topple over with your zombie. See you at the bottom.

#17
A ZOMBIE PIÑATA

Who ever invented the piñata is a genius. What's more awesome than stuffing a cardboard doll with candy and having kids beat the hell out of it? I know what's more awesome, tying up a zombie and having kids beat the hell out of it. Trust me, you won't fool anyone trying to pass off the zombie for a piñata, so just be honest. Tell the kids there's candy inside and let them go at it. When the kids are done and the zombie is nothing more than a lifeless body, just do what you would do with a regular piñata, toss it with the neighbor's trash.

Get him in the eye!

That's how you do it, kids.

One thing you have to keep in mind is in order to kill a zombie you gotta destroy the brain. The human brain is the most protected part on the body. I highly doubt that children could be able to break through the human skull. If after a few hours the zombie is still kicking, feel free to finish it off and keep the candy for yourself.

#18
DEATH BY BOOKS

No, I don't mean reading a terrible book (like this one) and bore it back to death. What I'm talking about is taking them to a public library or even a book store, look for the highest shelf with the biggest books. Tell your zombie to stay. When it stays you walk to the other side of the book shelf (look casual) and when no one is looking push the shelf on top of the zombie. Hopefully there will be enough books to destroy its brain. If not, then hopefully there are enough books to bury it so you can make a clean getaway.

Haha, later!

Fucking steroids aren't working!

The problem here is having enough strength to tip the bookshelf onto the zombie. Believe it or not, books are heavy. They're made out of paper, and paper is made out of trees. Trees are heavy, so in the end, books are heavy. If you can't push the bookshelf over, then abandon this method. It might work out better if you didn't push over a bookshelf. I'm sure you can get arrested for vandalism.

#19
THE WOOD CHIPPER

What a magnificent thing that wood chipper. If you live under a rock or are so wealthy that you never had to do landscaping, you won't know what a wood chipper is. Let me put it in easy terms. Cut down tree, shove it into one end of the machine and mulch comes out of the other end. Now replace tree with zombie. Cut up zombie, shove it into one end of the machine and mulch comes out of the other end. Who knows, you might discover that zombie is good fertilizer but not for plants. We learned earlier that that shit kills.

Fucking thing is loud.

Oh shit. My bad.

Before you think about doing this, make sure that you are in an open area. Last thing you want to do is have the mulch end pointed out into the street. You don't want to inadvertently infect other humans with the zombie virus. By the time you're done getting rid of one zombie, fifty more have already risen.

#20
TAR PIT

Tar pits or asphalt lakes as some people like to call them are good locations to rid yourself from a zombie. Animals sometimes get stuck in these things and end up dying. Years later, a fossilized version of animal remains can be excavated. Doesn't that sound cool? A fossilized version of a zombie! You might be asking, where are these tar pits? Well, I live in California and there are a few here. There's one in L.A., Bakersfield and Santa Barbara. Take your pick. When you push the zombie in make sure you laugh as you watch it struggle to get out.

"Relp Re, Ry Ruman."

Zaggerbots!

Now let's move forward into the future. It is 100 years later and you're long dead. Some archeologist decides to dig around that tar pit. There's no doubt they'll find your zombie friend, perfectly fresh. If the brain has not been destroyed, it should still be undead. When they fish it out, and then realize it's still functional, it'll be too late. That zombie will be so pissed it'll start eating everyone. It will start another zombie plague and it's your entire fault. But hey, who cares, you're already dead.

#21
TAKE IT TO ZUMMER CAMP

If you've been treating the zombie like it is part of the family then this method will work like a charm. When summer is approaching and you start thinking about sending your real kids to summer camp, start making plans to send your zombie as well. Just remember one important thing, you have to send your zombie to a different camp. If you're sending your kids to Camp Clean Lank, you send your zombie to Camp Krysty Lake. When summer is over, and your zombie's done singing campfire songs and trying to sneak into the girl's cabin, it's time to pick him up. Or is it? Just leave the zombie there and go pick up your real kids.

"Are you in the 5th grade, too?"

"You go in first."

When the zombie realizes no one is coming for it, there are two possible outcomes. One is that it will go on a rampage and start eating the counselors. The second is that it'll go into the woods and become the camp monster. Every camp has one, and you should be proud that your zombie has found a better life being the boogie-man. I can hear the stories now ... "There once was a zombie who drowned her kids."

#22
PUBLIC STORAGE

I see those public storage commercials all the time. I guess a zombie can be considered as "stuff". Well let's go for it. Call up one of these places and pay for one month. I say pay for a month because you'll only need the storage space for that long. Take the zombie and tell it to stay inside the storage room, say your goodbyes and lock the door. Never go back to that storage place.

In you go.

"Sold, to the man with the goggles for .52 cents!"

When the month is over and you've started ignoring the public storage calls, they will; in fact, sell your storage locker. Lucky for you the only thing in there is the zombie.

#23
MOSH PIT

If you're a fan of Death Metal then I suggest getting rid of your zombie by throwing it in the middle of a mosh pit. I've gone to a few shows and been in my share of pits. I know how dangerous they can be. A zombie's body is very frail and weak. There's no way that zombie will survive the perils of moshing.

"Fuck yeah!"

"Fuck yeah it hurts."

One thing you have to be careful of is the zombie's temper. These creatures get mad at everything. PMS to the millionth power. If someone starts shoving it, the zombie will fight back and even start biting. If this happens before the zombie is dismembered, be ready to get thrown out of the concert by security.

#24
METEORITE

What a perfect way to make sure every last bit of the zombie is destroyed. Everyone knows that meteors hit planet Earth all the time. Some are so small, they burn in the atmosphere before hitting the ground. In order for this to work you need to be very smart and know how to use gravity to make a meteor hit the Earth. I am not smart, at least not relativity smart. I know it's possible but actually doing it is beyond me.

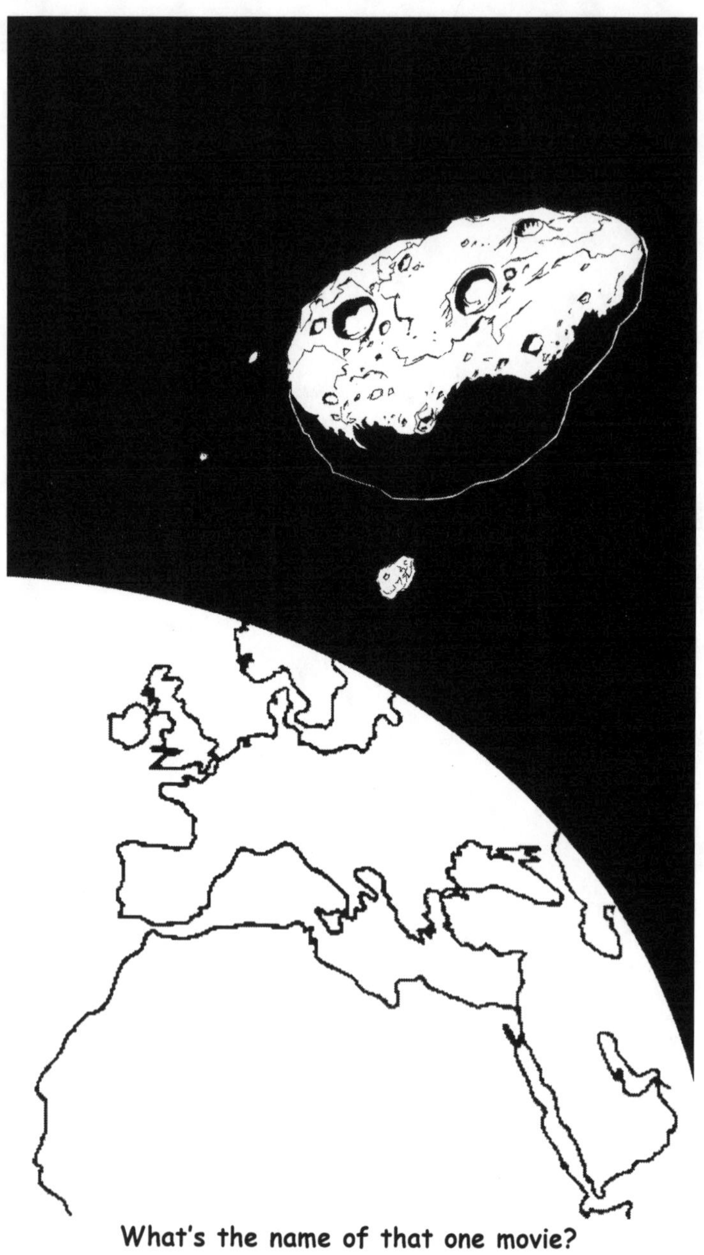

What's the name of that one movie?

. . .

Do us all a favor and use another method.

#25
GET THE ZOMBIE A JOB!

Don't we all wish house pets can pull their own weight? Having a dog get a job is a silly thought. Having a zombie get a job is also a silly thought, but it's more feasible. To do this, you have to get the newspaper. Sorry, for some reason I time traveled to pre-internet years. To do this, you have to get on the internet. Preferably Monster.com (pun!) and start posting your zombie's résumé. Maybe if you can actually land it a job and it starts bringing in some money, your wife might let you keep it.

"Stop eating the mouse, fucker!"

"Yeah, baby.
Why don't you dust the floor in front of me?"

If you can't find the zombie a job then do the next best thing. Put a French maid's uniform on it and tell your wife that you hired it to do some house cleaning. As much as everyone wants to see a zombie in a maid's uniform you still haven't gotten rid of the zombie. So if all else fails do #26.

#26
BEG!

When you've come to the conclusion how unrealistic these methods are, #26 will start looking like the best option. For everyone who's going to say, "But the title says 25 Ways to Get Rid of Your Zombie..." Shut your hole and I'll explain. #26 is not a way to get rid of your zombie. When everything else fails, (and it will) the only thing you can do is tell your wife that your zombie is here to stay. You tell her that you're the man of the house and that you bring home the bacon. Send her into the kitchen to fry you up some chicken.

"I said please, bitch!"

Should I just fuck the zombie?

When you finally come too and you're laid out on the front lawn with a black eye; remember, if you don't get rid of your zombie you'll more than likely join it. So, after your zombie helps you onto the city bus grab your credit card and rent a hotel. In the end your only real companion is your zombie friend.

I
MY ZOMBIE

OUTRODUCTION?

So, if this book has taught you anything, and I hope it hasn't, it's that you can have a lot of fun trying to get rid of a zombie. Some of these methods will take a lot of effort, but if you're dedicated and do them correctly, you will succeed in getting rid of your zombie.

Always keep in mind that you don't have to get rid of your zombie. I didn't, it's still here glaring at me as I write about the different ways to get rid of it. I hope it finally understands that it's my best friend and I'll always treasure that. But if it gets out of line I'd be happy to take it to Spain so it can run with the bulls ... I got an idea.

To be continued ...

ABOUT THE AUTHOR

Lyle Perez-Tinics (Writer/Editor/Publisher) is the creator of Undead in the Head Reviews a website dedicated to zombie books and the authors. He is the owner & Editor-in-Chief of Rainstorm Press and owner of The Mad Formatter, a book interior design business. He has stories in many anthologies and is currently working on two novels, Existing Dead and Rising from the Tempest. He is the mastermind behind The Undead That Saved Christmas charity anthology series.

Twitter - @LylePerez @RainstormPress
@UndeadintheHead

www.Facebook.com/RainstormPress

www.Facebook.com/UndeadintheHead

www.ExistingDead.com

BOOK FORMATTING FOR PRINT AND EBOOK.
$50.00 - $75.00 FOR PRINT BOOKS
$25.00 - $45.00 FOR EBOOK
Amazon Kindle, Smashwords and Barnes and Noble Pubit
"I've used the services of Lyle Perez-Tinics to format my novel. He has helped me on numerous occasions with formatting my stories in the past. Lyle's not only a great man to help improve your stories, but he's also a great guy to talk to. He's friendly, and will help with whatever you need added. In my opinion, you can't go wrong with talking to him."
- Lee Taylor, author of Morgue of the Dead
THE MAD FORMATTER

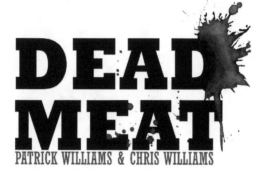

THE UNDEAD THAT SAVED CHRISTMAS VOL. 2

Another round of ghoulish holiday stories, **The Undead That Saved Christmas Vol. 2** is an anthology of both jolly and frightening proportions. From zombie toys to flesh-eating Santas, Vol. 2 is sure to be the most unique gift under the tree. The Undead That Saved Christmas Vol. 2 brings together various talented authors and artists from across the world.

Stories include: How I Got My Sack Back, by Stephen Johnston; Death and the Magi, by Joe McKinney; Zombies We Have Heard on High, by Jamie Freeman; You Better Watch Out, by Scott Morris, and others.

Get into the Christmas spirit with carols and poems such as 'Twas a Season of Zombies by Rebecca Besser and The Last Noel by Craig W. Chenery.

Whether you buy it for yourself, a friend, or family member, know you're doing it for a good cause. Proceeds from the sales of The Undead That Saved Christmas Vol. 2 benefit the Hugs Foster Family Agency (hugsffa.org) and will help them give their foster children gifts this holiday season. Introduction by Bud Hanzel and John Olson, authors of The Do-it-Yourself Guide to Surviving the Zombie Apocalypse.

Download a free sample at http://www.smashwords.com/books/view/105985

Available on Amazon, Barnes & Noble
eBook available on Amazon's Kindle, B&N's Nook, Smashwords.com

$14.95

ISBN: 978-1-93775-800-4 Library of Congress Control Number: 2011919478

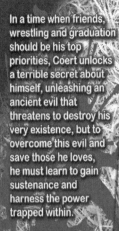